Mark Twain's

The Adventures of Huckleberry Finn

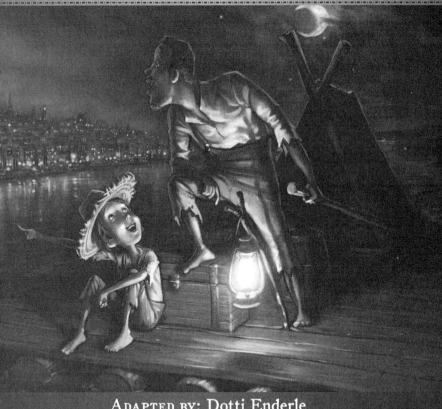

ADAPTED BY: Dotti Enderle
ILLUSTRATED BY: Howard McWilliam

magic
wagon

visit us at www.abdopublishing.com

Calico Chapter Books™ is a trademark and logo of Magic Wagon.

Printed in the United States of America, Melrose Park, Illinois
102009
012010

 PRINTED ON RECYCLED PAPER

Original text by Mark Twain
Adapted by Dotti Enderle
Illustrated by Howard McWilliam
Edited by Stephanie Hedlund and Rochelle Baltzer
Cover and interior design by Jaime Martens

Library of Congress Cataloging-in-Publication Data

Enderle, Dotti, 1954-
  The adventures of Huckleberry Finn / adapted by Dotti Enderle ;
illustrated by Howard McWilliam ; based on the works of Mark
Twain.
      p. cm. -- (Calico illustrated classics)
   ISBN 978-1-60270-702-3
  [1. Mississippi River--Fiction. 2. Voyages and travels--Fiction. 3.
Slavery--Fiction. 4. Missouri--History--19th century--Fiction. 5.
Friendship--Fiction.] I. McWilliam, Howard, 1977- ill. II. Twain,
Mark, 1835-1910. Adventures of Huckleberry Finn. III. Title.
   PZ7.E69645Ad 2010
   [Fic]--dc22
                                                    2009033489

Table of Contents

The Honest Truth

You don't know me unless you've read a book called *The Adventures of Tom Sawyer*. That book was written by Mr. Mark Twain. In it, Mr. Twain told the honest truth. Well, maybe he added a few extra things here and there.

Course it don't matter if you haven't heard of me. You'll be hearing a lot about me and my friend Tom Sawyer. Tom is my very best friend.

See, Tom and I had a wild time awhile back. We found a stash of gold that some robbers had hidden in a cave. And it was finder's keepers. Tom and I got $6,000 each. That's a heap of money!

Judge Thatcher put that money in the bank for us and gave us one dollar a day. That's a lot of money for me to spend in one day, but Tom can always think of something.

I lived by myself for a while because my pappy ran off. I had no idea where he went. But the Widow Douglas felt sorry for me and took me in to live with her. She thought I was some kind of savage and wanted to "civilize" me. She's always reminding me of my manners.

"Wash behind your ears, Huckleberry."

"Don't eat with your fingers, Huckleberry."

"Wipe your shoes before you come in, Huckleberry."

It seemed like she could never say my name without some reminder attached to it.

And she made me wear new clothes. They were itchy and tight, and I could barely breathe in them. I didn't think I could stand much more of her trying to make a gentleman of me.

Since I liked my old way of life, I snuck in my room, put on my old raggedy clothes, and ran away. I wasn't gone long before Tom hunted me down.

"You need to come back," Tom said.

"I ain't going back there," I told him, thinking how those shiny new shoes the widow gave me pinched my toes.

"You gotta come back, Huck," Tom said. "I'm thinking about starting a band of robbers. But I need you to be a part of it."

I scratched my chin. "I don't know, Tom. I hate the way the widow's always combing my hair."

"Do you want to be a robber or not?"

It did sound like a heap of fun. "All right. But can't I hide out somewhere and still be in your gang of robbers?"

"Nope. You have to go back to live with the Widow Douglas. Only respectable people can join up with us."

I didn't much like that plan, but I went back anyway.

⚜⚜

The widow cried when she saw me. "Oh, Huck, I was so worried. You are my poor lost

lamb." Then she called me a few bad names, but I know she didn't mean no harm. She put them fancy clothes back on me, and I felt all cramped up again.

Soon she rang the bell for supper. I knew I couldn't dillydally. When she rang that bell, she expected me to come down on time. And when I got to the table, I had to wait until the widow grumbled a prayer.

After supper the widow got out her book and read to me about Moses. He seemed awful adventurous. But then she told me that Moses had been dead for a long, long time. I didn't really care about listening anymore cause I don't take much stock in dead people.

The widow's sister, Miss Watson, came to live with her. She was a skinny old maid who always looked down on me with her glasses perched on the end of her nose. Miss Watson thought she could educate me.

She'd set me down, pull out a spelling book, and work me hard for about an hour. Then the

Widow Douglas would come to my rescue. "I think he's had enough spelling lessons for today," she'd say.

Then the next hour would be deadly dull. I couldn't help but fidget. Miss Watson would get onto me about it.

"Don't put your feet up there, Huckleberry."

"Don't scrunch up like that, Huckleberry—set up straight."

Then she'd say, "Try to behave yourself. Huckleberry, if you don't mind your manners, you'll go down to the bad place."

"That's okay with me," I told her. "I'm powerful bored and could use a change."

"Oh, Huckleberry, that's a wicked thing to say!"

I didn't want to tell her that I'd go just about any place to get away from her.

Once everybody had gone to bed, I snuck out for a spell. The stars were shining, and the leaves rustled in the woods. I heard an owl who-whooing in a tree. It gave me cold shivers.

Then way out in the woods I heard the kind of sound that a ghost makes when it can't rest easy in the grave. That's when I got plumb scared. I was wishing I had someone to keep me company.

I was shaking all over when I heard the town clock go *boom–boom–boom*—twelve times. It seemed everything was still. The wind had stopped blowing. The crickets had stopped chirping. That's when I heard a twig snap down in the darkest part of the trees.

Something was stirring. I sat real still and listened. Soon I heard a *me-yow! me-yow!* I said, "Me-yow! Me-yow!" right back as soft as I could.

I got up and went over by the shed. Sure enough, just as I suspected, there was Tom Sawyer waiting for me.

The Band of Robbers

Tom and I went tiptoeing along the path. When we passed the kitchen, we saw Jim, one of Miss Watson's slaves, standing in the doorway. We crouched down real still.

Jim stretched his neck out and said, "Who's there?" He listened some more, and then he came tiptoeing down the path, too.

Tom and I stayed real still. Jim was so close we could reach out and touch him. But I started itching. First my ankle, then my ear, and next my back. I was itching so bad, but I didn't dare scratch. It was mighty painful. But pretty soon Jim lay down under a tree, and we heard him snoring.

"Let's play a trick on him," Tom said.

"What kind of trick?" I asked. I didn't think that was a very good idea. But Tom was hankering to do some mischief, so he took Jim's hat off his head and hung it on a tree limb.

We left him snoozing under the tree, then snuck back into the house to snatch some candles.

We cut along the path until we came to the hill. Joe Harper, Ben Rogers, and a couple of other boys were waiting there. We went over to a clump of bushes, and Tom made everybody swear to keep a secret. He showed us a hole on the side of the hill.

We crawled in on our hands and knees until the cave opened up wider.

"Now we'll start this band of robbers," Tom said. "We'll call it Tom Sawyer's Gang."

We all nodded because nobody wanted to argue with Tom.

"Everybody who wants to join up has to take an oath," he went on.

We all nodded again.

"And," Tom said, "we each have to write our name in blood."

I wasn't too happy about that part, but Tom got out a sheet of paper. He wrote the oath on it and read it out loud. "Everyone has to swear that they'll stick with the gang, and never tell our secrets, or we'll harm that boy's family."

They turned to look at me. Then Ben Rogers said, "But Huck Finn ain't got no family."

"That's true," Tom said.

I started getting nervous. I wanted to be in Tom's band of robbers. It wasn't fair that I'd get kicked out because my pappy left me.

Tom let out a mournful sigh. "Sorry, Huck. Looks like you can't be in the gang."

I was ready to cry. It just didn't seem right. Then I said, "How about Miss Watson? If I spill any secrets, you can go after her."

Tom nodded. "All right. She'll do."

We all stuck pins in our fingers to swear the blood oath. Then I asked, "Who are we going to rob?"

"We're not exactly robbers," Tom said. "We'll kidnap people and hold them for ransom."

We all looked at each other. "What's a ransom?" I asked.

"I don't know," Tom said, "but that's what they do in some of the books I've read. So that's what we'll do."

I scratched my head. "But how can we do it if we don't know what it is?"

Tom thought on that for a spell. "Maybe ransom means you keep people hid until they're dead. We'll keep them tied up here."

"But won't that be a bother?" I asked. "They'll be eating our food and trying to get loose. It sounds like a lot of work."

"Then we'll have a guard look after them," he answered. That sounded like a pretty good idea.

We kept on talking about our plans, and after a while one of the boys fell asleep. When we woke him up, he cried and said he wanted his ma and that he didn't want to be a robber anymore.

The other boys made fun of him, calling him a crybaby. That only made him cry louder. But Tom gave him five cents to keep quiet, and we let him go.

After that I snuck back to the widow's house. My new clothes were all greased up and grimy and I was dog-tired.

Miss Watson scolded me when she saw what I'd done to my nice clothes, but the widow was nice about it. She cleaned off the dirt, and she looked so sad about it that I decided I would behave for a while.

A few days later some folks said they found my pappy. I was scared at first. When I lived with him, I spent most of my time hiding in the woods. Pap drank a lot, and whipped me with a stick. I didn't want no more of that.

But then I heard that they had found a body floating in the river. They figured it was Pap. No one could recognize his face, but they said it was him anyway because of his size and his ragged clothes. They buried him on the bank.

I got to thinking about it. I figured if it wasn't Pap, he might just turn up again, though I was really wishing he wouldn't.

CHAPTER
3

Bad Luck

Three or four months passed, and it was well into the winter. I'd spent most of that time in school. I learned to spell and read, and I could write a little, too.

I'd also learned to say my multiplication tables up to six times seven is thirty-five. I don't reckon I could learn it any higher than that even if I lived forever.

At first I hated the school, but eventually I learned to like it some. And the longer I went to school, the easier it got.

I was getting used to the widow's ways, too. Living in a house and sleeping in a warm bed seemed pretty nice in the winter months. I liked the old ways best, but it was getting so I liked the new ones too . . . a little bit. The widow said I was doing real fine and that she wasn't ashamed of me at all.

One morning I accidentally turned over the saltshaker at breakfast. I reached for some of it as quick as I could to throw over my left shoulder. If I didn't, I'd have some powerful bad luck. But Miss Watson was there, and she scolded me good.

"Don't worry about it," the Widow Douglas said. She cleaned up the mess before I had a chance to throw a pinch of salt over my shoulder. Now I'd have bad luck for sure.

I went down to the front garden and climbed over the fence. There was an inch of new snow on the ground. I was feeling a bit shaky about my luck. What bad thing could happen? It didn't take long for me to find out.

I saw some footprints in the snow. Someone had stood by the garden fence. But why would they just stand there looking? Why didn't they come up and knock on the door?

I stooped down to get a closer look. At first I didn't notice anything strange, but then I saw it. There was a cross in the left boot heel made out of big nails. It was a superstition to ward off the devil.

I didn't waste no time running down the hill. I looked over my shoulder every now and then to see if I was being followed. Nobody was there. I made it to Judge Thatcher's place as quick as I could.

"Why, boy, you're out of breath," he said. "Did you come for some of your money?"

"No, sir," I told him. "Is there some for me?"

He chuckled. "Yes, Huck, but maybe you should let me invest it for you instead of spending it."

"No sir," I said. "I don't want to invest it or spend it. I don't want it at all. I want you to take it. It's all yours."

He looked surprised. "I don't understand. Why would you want to give it away?"

"Don't ask me no questions, Judge Thatcher. Just take it, please."

He scratched his head. "Well, I'm puzzled. Is something the matter?"

"Just take it, and don't ask me about it. That way I won't have to tell any lies."

He studied on it awhile. "Oh, I think I see. You want to sell all your property to me, not give it away. I'll pay you one dollar."

Then he wrote something on a sheet of paper and said, "There, you see? It says 'for a

consideration.' That means I have bought it from you and paid for it. Here's a dollar. Now you sign the paper."

It sounded like a square deal to me, so I signed it and left.

When I got back to the widow's house, I went straight back to see Jim. He could see I was upset.

"What's wrong, Huck?"

"My pappy's come back. I saw his tracks in the snow."

Jim pulled out a hair ball that had come out of the stomach of an ox. It was about the size of my fist. Jim said it had magic powers.

"What is it you want to know?" he asked me.

"I was wondering what Pap's going to do, and if he plans on staying."

Jim whispered over the hair ball. Then he dropped it on the floor. It bounced once and then rolled about an inch. Jim tried it again, but the same thing happened. So Jim got down on the floor and put his ear to it.

"It ain't talking," he said. "But, sometimes the hair ball speaks better if you give it money."

I reached in my pocket and pulled out a quarter. It wasn't a real quarter, but I figured the hair ball wouldn't know that.

Jim smelled the quarter, bit down on it, and rubbed it. "I think we can trick it with this."

He placed the fake quarter under the hair ball and got down to listen again. Then Jim spoke in a mysterious voice, "Your pappy don't know what he's going to do. Sometimes he thinks he'll go away, and sometimes he figures he'll stay. It's better to wait and see what he does."

I wasn't much for waiting, but that's what the hair ball told me to do. I was plumb tired that night so I lit a candle and went up to my room. When I opened the door, my heart stood still and my breath hitched. Right there sat Pap, giving me an evil grin.

Trapped

I shut the door and turned around. I had always been scared of Pap for tanning my hide so much. But I realized that there was nothing to be scared of now.

Pap was almost fifty, and he looked it. His hair was long and tangled and greasy. It was deep black, and so was his scruffy whiskers. What I could make out of his face was ghostly white. His clothes were nothing but rags.

He sat with his chair tilted back, looking at me. I noticed the window was open. He'd gotten up on the shed and climbed in.

"Starchy clothes," he said. "Guess you think you're some big deal, huh?"

"Maybe I am, maybe I ain't."

"Don't give me none of your lip, boy. I hear you're educated now. They say you can read and write. You think you're better than your own father now? Who told you that you could mingle with the fine folks?"

"The widow told me," I said to him.

"Well, I'll teach the widow a thing or two. You ain't got no business up here with fancy clothes and a soft bed to sleep in."

I didn't say nothing cause I just wanted him to leave. Then he said, "If you really can read, then show me."

I picked up a book about George Washington and started reading. I could see the fire in his eyes now. He grabbed the book from my hands and flung it across the room.

"I hear that you're rich now. That's why I came back. You go get that money for me tomorrow. I want it."

"But I don't have that money anymore."

He pointed his filthy finger at me. "That's a lie! I know Judge Thatcher has it. You get it from him and give it to me."

"I ain't got no money," I said. "Ask Judge Thatcher. He'll tell you."

"All right," he agreed. "I will. But right now, you can give me what's in your pocket."

"I only have a dollar, and I need that to—"

He didn't let me finish. "I don't care what you need it for. Hand it over."

I gave it to him. He climbed back out the window and hopped over onto the shed. And then he was gone.

I heard that the next day he visited Judge Thatcher. He tried to bully him into giving up the money. Judge Thatcher wouldn't give in. Pap said that money was rightfully his, and that he'd force the judge to hand it over. That's when Judge Thatcher and the Widow Douglas decided they needed to protect me.

They tried to sign some papers that would give the Widow Douglas the full right to raise me. And the papers said that Pap couldn't come to see me anymore. But there was a new judge in town who wouldn't listen. He said a boy should be with his father. He decided he would take Pap in and make a better man of him. That's like trying to train a skunk not to stink.

The new judge took Pap to his house. Pap bathed and put on some new clothes. He got cleaned up real nice.

That judge taught Pap some manners. Then he had Pap put his mark on a piece of paper, promising that he'd always be a better man. But that night, Pap got powerful thirsty. He sold his fancy coat for a jug of whiskey and drank it until he passed out.

The judge was pretty mad about the whole thing. He wanted to take Pap back to his house and try again, but Pap held a shotgun on him. He said he'd never go back.

Pretty soon Pap was up to his old business. He aimed to get that money, so he went to the courts to make Judge Thatcher give it up. Pap

also came around a lot, telling me not to go to school. I went anyway, just to make him mad.

One day Pap saw me outside. I tried to run, but he caught me. He took me about three miles up the river. He locked me in an old log hut.

He kept me with him all the time so I couldn't run away. And every once in a while, Pap would get a switch and whip me good.

Lots of times, Pap would lock me in the hut and go away. Sometimes I worried that he might've drowned, and I'd never get away. I tried to find a way out, but the windows were so small that even a coon couldn't slip through.

Pap was pretty careful not to leave a knife or anything in the cabin while he was gone. But, I finally found something that would work. Up in the rafters was a rusty saw. It didn't have a handle, but that was fine with me. I got it down and I started sawing hard.

Escape

I heard Pap coming up from town, so I hid the saw again and waited. Pap stormed in, yelling and pitching a fit. "You can't trust the government! You can't trust lawyers!"

I sat back, waiting. He was so grouchy I was afraid he'd take a stick to me.

"That $6,000 is mine!" He was screeching louder than an owl caught by a wild dog. "And I could get it if they'd ever start that stupid trial! You know what that lawyer told me? He said even when I get that money, the widow will still try to take you back to live with her."

I started thinking about my fancy clothes and shiny shoes. I'd gotten used to these old rags again.

"She can't have you!" he bellowed. "You're my son!" He piped down a little and looked at me with those dark eyes of his. "Get on out to the boat and fetch the supplies I brought from town."

I didn't argue one bit. It was good to be outside again, even if it was for just a few minutes. I looked down at the things he'd gotten. There was a sack of cornmeal, a side of bacon, and a large jug of whiskey. I toted them up to the cabin, and then went back down to bring the boat up on the shore so it wouldn't wash away.

I looked back at the cabin, and then over at the woods. If I wanted to, I could take off running right now. I'd just keep going as far away as my feet would carry me. But that's when Pap yelled, "Boy, are you asleep or drowned?"

I trudged back up to the cabin. By then it was nearly dark.

I was cooking our supper when the old man started drinking. He still kept on yelping about the government. He was fighting mad. But after a while, he'd drank too much and fell asleep right there on the floor.

I figured I could sneak over and take the key from his pocket, but he was having a restless sleep. He kept moaning and rolling around. I knew it was no use. I waited and waited for him to settle down, but then I got too tired. I just couldn't keep my eyes open, and I fell asleep.

It was after sunup when Pap woke me. "Get out there and catch us some fish," he ordered.

I grabbed my pole and headed out. The water in the river was running swift, and all kinds of branches and bark were floating downstream. I knew then that the water had risen.

I was about to throw my fishing line in when I saw something else floating toward me. It was a canoe.

I couldn't let it pass by. I jumped in and swam over to it. It was empty inside. I thought, *Pap will love this. I bet it's worth ten dollars.* But then I had a better idea.

I pulled that canoe up on the banks and hid it behind some bushes. When I had my chance, I'd paddle the canoe down the river and set up camp. No one would ever find me.

"Where've you been, and why are you so wet?" Pap fussed when I got back.

"I fell in the river."

He grumped around awhile, and then locked me inside the cabin again. Once he set off for town, I had my chance.

I pulled the saw out of its hiding place and started cutting into the cabin wall again. It took awhile, but I finally cut a good size hole. I could've run off right then, but I didn't figure that would be a good idea. Pap would know I'd run off, and he'd come looking for me.

So I grabbed the ax outside and smashed the door with it. Then I found a wild hog lying dead in the woods. I put it in an old cornmeal sack and dripped some of its blood on the cabin floor. I pulled out some of my hair and dropped it on the floor, too.

I dragged the sack out of the cabin and down to the river. I made it look like someone had killed me and took me away. If Pap thought I was dead, he wouldn't bother me anymore.

I grabbed some food and supplies and didn't waste another minute. I hopped in the canoe and let it float down the river, carrying me away.

Several miles downstream, I came up on Jackson Island. It was right in the middle of the river. I steered the canoe up on the bank and breathed in the fresh air. It felt good to be free at last.

After a while I fetched my things from the canoe. I made a tent out of my blankets in case it rained. Near sundown I made a campfire. I caught a fish for my supper and an extra one for my breakfast. Then I lay back and counted the stars.

I was there for about three days, hunting and fishing and just being lazy. But on the third day, I saw smoke coming from the other side of the island. I slipped through the trees and carefully made my way over to see if it was robbers or thieves.

I stayed behind some bushes at first, but then I decided to get a closer look. I saw a man stretched out with a blanket around his head. I snuck up real quiet and waited. Pretty soon he stretched, and that blanket came off. That's when I saw his face. It was Miss Watson's slave.

"Hello, Jim!" I said.

Adventuring

Jim bounced up and stared at me with wild eyes. Then he dropped down on his knees, and put his hands together, saying, "Don't hurt me! Please don't! I've never done any harm to a ghost. I've always liked dead people. Go get back in the river where you belong."

"Jim, I ain't dead," I told him.

He poked my side and touched my arm. "You ain't dead," he said, happy to see me.

I was just as happy to see him. It was getting mighty lonesome on this island. I looked down at his campfire. "Let's make some breakfast."

After we ate, we lay back for a bit. Jim asked, "Huck, if you're here, then who was killed back at that hut?"

I told him the whole story.

"That's pretty smart," he said. "Even Tom Sawyer couldn't come up with a better plan than that."

"But what about you, Jim? How'd you end up here?"

He squirmed, looking uneasy. "Maybe I better not tell."

"Why not?" I asked.

"You wouldn't tell on me, would you?" he asked.

"I swear I won't."

Jim leaned closer to me. "I run off."

"Jim!"

"Now, Huck, you said you wouldn't tell."

"Yeah, I swore," I said, "and I'll stick to it."

"The thing is," he tells me, "Miss Watson always said she'd never sell me. But the other night I heard her tell the widow that she didn't really want to, but she could sell me for $800."

"That's a lot of money," I said.

"The widow tells Miss Watson she shouldn't do it, but I didn't wait to hear what Miss Watson had to say. I climbed down the hill, stole a boat, and here I am."

"Well, I'm glad you're here," I told him.

We stayed by the campfire for a while, then Jim started looking at the sky. The birds were flocked together, flying away.

"A storm's coming," Jim said. "It's going to be a bad one."

I looked at our blankets, the only protection we had. "We can't stay out here."

"Come on, Huck, I'll show you something." That's when he led me to a small cave. Jim thought it was a bit cramped for two people, but I just said it was cozy. We spread blankets inside for a carpet and ate our dinner in there.

Pretty soon that storm rolled in. It got so dark everything looked blue-black outside. The thunder crashed and the lightning slashed across the sky. And it rained like all fury.

The rain thrashed along so thick, the trees looked dim and spiderwebby. And the wind rushed so hard it would bend those trees like they were twigs.

"Jim, this is nice," I said. "I wouldn't want to be no place else but here. Pass me some more of that cornbread."

"Yeah, well, you wouldn't be in here if it weren't for me," he reminded me.

We stayed in there until the storm passed and it was safe to wander out.

The river went on rising and rising. Before long it was over the banks. During the day, we'd paddle all through the island in the canoe. It was cool and shady in the deep woods even if the sun was blazing down.

We went winding in and out among the trees. Sometimes the vines hung so thick we had to back up and go another way. And we saw all kinds of rabbits and snakes and turtles.

But the water kept rising, and all manner of things went drifting along. One night we saw a little section of a raft with nice pine planks. It was twelve feet wide and about fifteen or sixteen feet long. It was a solid level floor.

In the daytime we'd see logs floating by, but we'd just let them go. We didn't want to show ourselves in the daylight.

Then another night, we were up at the head of the island. Just before daybreak, we saw a wood frame house that had been carried down by the water. It was a two-story, and tilted over some. We paddled out to it.

There was a window sticking up, so we tried peeking in.

"Look at that," I said to Jim.

We tried to see if there was anything we could take. There were two old chairs inside, but we didn't have any use for them. There was a bed in the corner. It was stripped of bedding so it wasn't any use either. Then we saw some clothes hanging on the wall.

"Maybe we can take some of those," I said.

"Why would we need those clothes?" Jim asked. "I'm just fine with what I'm wearing."

"But we might need them for rags."

Jim nodded. "Yeah, that is a good idea."

We slipped through that window. It wasn't easy considering the water was bobbing the house up and down.

"You go grab some of those clothes," Jim said, "and I'll see if there's anything else we can use."

I did just what he said. I started pulling clothes off that wall and bundling them up. "Jim! You find anything else?"

"Nope," he said. "I guess we'll just make do with these rags."

We hurried back to the window to climb out, but that's when I saw something through the door of the next room. There were feet poking out from behind a bed.

"Jim," I whispered.

He looked over and saw it too. "Hello, you!" Jim hollered. The man didn't move. "Hey!" he hollered again. But the man stayed still as a rod.

Jim looked at me, his eyes wide. "Huck, I don't think that man's asleep."

I felt a chill spike right through me. Jim was right, that man wasn't asleep. He was right out dead!

Sarah Williams

"You think he's really dead?" I asked, looking at the man's feet poking out.

"I'll check," Jim said. He went back in and bent down by the bed. "He's dead all right."

Jim looked up at me. "He's been shot in the back. Looks like he's been dead for a day or two."

I took a step inside the room, but Jim said, "Don't come no closer, Huck. Don't look at his face. It's too ghastly."

He didn't have to tell me twice. I decided I didn't want to look at a dead man's face anyway.

Jim threw some old rags over the man in case I decided to take a peek after all. The room was a giant mess. There was a heap of greasy poker-playing cards scattered around the floor. The walls had filthy words written on them.

We found some women's dresses and a sunbonnet hanging up in the room. There were some men's clothes too, and an old tin lantern, a butcher knife with no handle, and a brand-new jackknife.

The way they were scattered, we figured whoever lived here must of took off in a hurry. We grabbed an old bed quilt and a tin cup that was laying there. We gathered as much as we could and put it in the canoe. We'd made a pretty good haul.

By the time we shoved off, it was already daylight. So I made Jim lie down in the canoe and cover up with the quilt so he wouldn't be seen. I paddled us home safe and sound.

After breakfast I wanted to talk about the dead man, but Jim said to forget it. He claimed it would bring us bad luck, and he didn't want any ghosts hanging around.

We rummaged through the clothes and found eight dollars sewed up inside one of the shirts. Jim said the money was probably stolen. But that didn't matter. Now it was ours.

The next day I was getting restless and wanted to paddle the canoe across the river to see what was going on over there. Jim came up with a clever idea.

"Here, Huck," he said, "put these on." He handed over one of the dresses that we'd gotten from that old house.

"Why would I want to wear this?" I asked.

"So that nobody'll recognize you if you're seen."

That seemed like a pretty sound idea to me. Jim tugged that dress over my head and buttoned it up, and I rolled my trouser legs up to my knees. Then Jim placed the sunbonnet on my head and tied it under my chin. He stepped back and looked me over.

"Huck, you look just like a girl. Ain't nobody going to recognize you even in the daylight."

I practiced walking around to get the hang of it. Jim said I didn't walk like a girl, and that I should stop hiking my dress up to get to my trouser pockets. I practiced some more and did better. Then when it got dark, I hopped in the canoe and headed up the shore.

I crossed over to the edge of town and started up along the bank. I saw a light burning in an old cabin. I slipped up and peeked in the window. There was a woman inside, knitting by candlelight.

She was a stranger, which was lucky for me. Even though I was dressed like a girl, I didn't want anyone to recognize my voice. I knocked on the door.

"Come in," the woman said. So I did.

"Take a chair," she told me. I sat down next to her.

She looked me over with her shiny eyes. "And what might your name be?"

I had to think up something fast. "Sarah Williams."

"Do you live in the neighborhood?" she asked me.

"No, ma'am. I live in Hookerville, about seven miles away. I've walked all this way, and I'm pretty tired."

"And hungry, too, I reckon," she said.

"I ain't hungry. I ate not long ago. But my mother is really sick, and we're out of money, so I walked all this way to tell my uncle, Abner Moore. Do you know him?"

"No, but I've only lived here for two weeks." Then she said, "You better spend the night."

"No, I'd rather just rest awhile, and then go on. I ain't afraid of the dark."

But she wouldn't let me leave. "You can't go. My husband will be home in an hour or so, and I'm sure he'd want to meet you."

She went on talking about her husband and how and why they'd moved here. I was starting to think I'd made a mistake by coming. But then she started talking about something else that really stirred my blood. She knew all about me and Tom Sawyer and the money we'd gotten! Only she said it was $10,000 instead of $6,000.

"Yes," she said. "And that poor boy. His pappy was a hard old man. He took that boy away, and next thing you know, the boy is murdered. He never had a chance."

"Who done it?" I asked. I wanted to see what other folks knew about me and Pap.

"Some thought old man Finn did it himself, but that same night a slave ran away. They think it was the slave that killed him. Folks are out hunting for him right now, and there's a $300 reward for whoever finds him."

All that talk gave me the jitters. I needed to look busy, so I took up a needle off the table and tried to thread it. My hands shook, and I wasn't doing a very good job. The woman smiled at me so I put the needle back down.

She kept looking at me pretty curious. Then she said, "What did you say your name was, honey?"

"M—Mary Williams."

"I thought you said your name was Sarah."

"Yes, ma'am. Mary is my middle name."

"Come on," she egged. "What's your real name? Is it Bill or Tom or Bob? What is it?"

I was shaking like a leaf. I didn't know what to say. "How'd you know I was a boy?"

"'Cause when you thread a needle, you're supposed to hold it still and put the thread through. You did just the opposite. Now tell me your real name."

"George Peters," I lied.

"Well, trot along now Sarah Mary Williams George Peters. And if you get into any trouble, just send word to me, Mrs. Judith Loftus."

I rushed out and hopped into the canoe. I had to get back to Jim. I knew now that there were folks out there looking for him just to get that $300 reward.

Afloat

When I got back, I made a campfire at the edge of the island. Then I ran to the cavern and woke Jim.

"They're after you!" I said. "We've got to get going."

Jim smelled the smoke and asked. "Why'd you build a fire?"

"Because it'll lead them here. When they see you're gone, they'll wait for you to come back. That'll keep them here for a few days."

"That's a real good plan, Huck."

We didn't bother with the canoe. We loaded everything onto a stray raft that had floated up when the river flooded. Then we got on and sailed off.

Jim took some planks and built a snug wigwam to keep us and our supplies good and dry. We made an extra steering oar in case the other one broke. And we fixed up a short forked stick to hang our lantern on. We knew to light that lantern when a steamboat came by so it wouldn't run over us.

We loved drifting on the big river. At night, we'd lay back and look up at the stars. Sometimes we'd pass small towns, their lights twinkling like fireflies. But on our fifth night, we passed by St. Louis. It was like the whole world lit up.

The night we passed St. Louis, a big storm came up. Jim and I stayed inside the wigwam and let the raft steer itself. When the lightning flashed, we could see the big straight river ahead and high rocky bluffs on each side.

"Hey, Jim, look over yonder!"

There was a steamboat that had crashed onto the rocks. We were drifting straight for it.

"I want to go onboard," I said to Jim. "It would be an adventure. Tom Sawyer would do it. Besides, we might find some more supplies."

Jim grumbled a little, and then he gave in.

We slipped on and made our way to the captain's door. We could see a light and hear voices inside.

"I think we should scoot out of here fast," Jim whispered.

"Yep," I agreed. "Let's go."

But before we turned away, I heard a voice wailing and begging, "Oh, please don't, boys! I swear I won't ever tell!"

Jim had already headed for the raft, but I was too curious. I thought, *Tom Sawyer wouldn't back out, so I won't either.* I dropped down on my hands and knees and crept forward.

I saw a man stretched out on the floor. His hands and feet were tied. There were two men standing over him. One held a lantern, the other held a pistol.

The man on the floor kept begging, "Please, I won't tell anyone!"

Every time he'd say that, the man with the lantern grinned. "Indeed you ain't!"

The man with the pistol was ready to shoot, but the other man said, "Wait!" They mumbled a few things, and then headed my way.

I scooted out of there quick as I could and hid behind some boxes. Then the two men stood talking at the deck rail.

"Let's just put the loot in our boat and head out," one man said. "It won't be long before this steamboat washes back into the river and sinks. When it does, old Jim Turner in there will drown for sure."

"But suppose it doesn't wash back out?" the other man said.

"I guess we can wait a bit to see."

When they headed back in, I lit out. I was covered in a cold sweat.

"Jim," I whispered, "there's a gang of murderers yonder. We need to find their boat so we can cut it loose. Then they'll be stuck here. The sheriff will be able to find them and take them in. We've got to hurry. You look on one side, and I'll look on the other."

"And then what, Huck?"

"What do you think? We'll get back on the raft and sail out of here."

Jim let out a powerful sigh. "We can't, Huck. There ain't no raft. It broke loose and sailed off on its own. We're stuck here."

The Grangerfords

Well, here we were, stranded on the steamboat with those two evil men inside.

"We've got to find their boat now," I told Jim. "We need it for ourselves."

Jim was so scared he was quaking. I had the jitters, too. But we had to keep our heads about us. It was slow work, but soon we found their small boat tied up on the side.

I was ready to hop in when the door opened and one of the men poked his head out. He was only about two feet from me. I held my breath, not daring to move. But then he went back in and said, "Bring that lantern here, Bill!"

I didn't waste time waiting for him to come back out. Jim and I hopped in that boat and quickly cut the rope. We pushed off and headed down the river, looking for our raft.

We drifted along for several miles before we spotted it and climbed aboard. It felt good being back with our supplies and the wigwam.

We floated along for about three days. Then the river opened up and we knew we were heading in the right direction. We wanted to get to Cairo, a town on the Ohio River. It was a free state, and Jim would no longer be a slave there. But we had to be careful not to pass it.

Jim hid in the wigwam during the day. We couldn't take a chance on him being seen. But one day I spotted a couple of men heading our way. When they got close enough one said, "Hey, boy, are you alone?"

"No, sir."

"Well, we're after five runaway slaves. Is your other passenger black or white?"

"White," I said. There was no way I'd tell them otherwise.

"Maybe we should come aboard and check," one of them said to me.

"Sure, but my pap is powerful sick."

"What's wrong with him?" the man asked.

I had to think quick. "He's got smallpox," I lied. "Can you help him?"

Well, those fellows started steering away quick. "Stay away from us!" they hollered. They headed off ahead of us, and I was plenty glad to see them go.

It was later that night when a fog rolled in as thick as gravy. Even with our lantern, Jim and I couldn't see a thing. But we heard something paddling behind us.

"Jim, that's a steamboat heading our way!"

Jim's eyes grew big as he looked at me. "What're we going to do, Huck?"

There wasn't nothing we could do. The lights on that steamboat were like halos in the fog. And they couldn't see our lantern.

Pretty soon it hit, breaking our raft apart like it was a bundle of twigs. I grabbed a plank and held on. The waves of the steamboat washed me toward the shore. I made it onto the bank, but Jim was nowhere around.

I walked about a quarter mile when I saw a house up ahead. I was going to rush by it, but some dogs jumped out and went to howling and barking at me. I stood still, knowing not to move an inch.

A few seconds later a man poked his head out the window. "Who's there?" he asked.

I had to think up another fake name. "George Jackson, sir."

"What do you want?" he asked me.

"I just want to be moving along, but these dogs won't let me." They'd stopped barking but kept their eyes trained on me.

The man poked his head out a little more. "Why are you prowling at this time of night?"

"I wasn't prowling around, sir. I fell overboard off the steamboat." It was another lie, but it was better than having those dogs tear me apart.

"What'd you say your name was?" he asked again.

"George Jackson, sir. I'm only a boy."

"Is there anybody with you?"

"No, sir, nobody."

He came out, holding a candle. "Boy, do you know the Shepherdsons?"

"No, sir. I've never heard of them."

He held the candle closer. He looked me up and down. "Well, you don't look like a Shepherdson. Come on in."

There were three men and a gray-haired old lady inside. Behind her were two young women. The whole family looked handsome.

"Bless you," the old woman said. "You're as wet as can be. And I reckon you're hungry, too."

Soon they were sitting me at their table and feeding me cold cornpone, corned beef, and buttermilk. I'd never tasted anything so good.

Then a boy came in, rubbing the sleep from his eyes. "What's going on?" he asked.

"Buck, this is George Jackson," the woman said. "Take George upstairs and get him some dry clothes."

Buck looked to be about my age—thirteen

or fourteen. He was a little bigger than me though. I followed Buck up, and pretty soon I was dressed. I decided right then that they were the nicest family I'd ever seen. I was invited to stay with them awhile.

I soon learned that the family's name was Grangerford. Colonel Grangerford was a fine, upstanding man. There was also Bob, the oldest, and then Tom. Their sister, Miss Charlotte, was about twenty-five years old. And the other sister, Sophia, was as kind and gentle as a dove.

A few days later, Buck and I were out in the woods together when we heard someone coming up on a horse.

"Quick," Buck said. "Hide in the bushes."

We crouched down, peeking out through the leaves. A man sitting high on his horse came galloping by. I figured we'd just let him pass, but what happened next made my blood run cold. Buck pulled up his rifle and fired.

The Feud

I nearly jumped out of my skin when Buck's gun went off. So did the other fellow. The bullet hit his hat, and it went flying right off his head. The man grabbed his gun and went chasing after us.

Buck and I ran through the woods. I kept looking over my shoulder in case I needed to dodge a bullet. Finally the man turned back, to get his hat I reckon, and we kept running till we were back home.

We sat out under some vines, and I was so out of breath I could barely speak.

"Who was that?" I asked Buck.

"That was Harney Shepherdson," he said.

"And you wanted to kill him?"

Buck nodded. "You bet I did."

I scratched my head. "What'd he ever do to you?" I asked.

"Him?" Buck said. "He never done nothing to me."

"Well, then, why'd you want to kill him?"

Buck leaned back and pulled his knees up. "Because of the feud."

"You're in a feud with the Shepherdsons?"

"Yep," he said. "We've been in a feud since I can remember."

"Why?" I asked.

He thought on that a minute. "I reckon I don't know."

"Well, who started it? Was it a Grangerford or a Shepherdson?"

"How would I know?"

"Does anybody know?" I asked.

Buck shrugged. "Pa might know. He's gotten a few buckshot in him. And Bob has been cut with a knife. Tom's been hurt once or twice, too."

I had to wrap my mind around that. These families were fighting, and no one could remember why.

The next Sunday we all went to church. The men took their guns. They kept them resting between their knees during the service. I looked around and saw the Shepherdsons were doing the same. It seemed kind of silly seeing as the sermon was about brotherly love.

About an hour after dinner, everybody was dozing in their chairs. Miss Sophia stood in her doorway, motioning for me to come over. I looked around, wondering why she wanted to talk to me. When I walked into her room, she shut the door.

"Would you do me a favor?" she asked.

I liked her a lot, so naturally I said yes.

"I left my Bible laying at the church. Would you slip out quietly and go fetch it for me? But please don't tell anybody."

"Yes, ma'am," I said.

I slid out of there and off up the road. When I got to the church, no one was there. I went on in and found her Bible. But when I picked it up, a slip of paper fell out with *Half-past two* written on it in pencil. I placed it back in the Bible and left.

When I got back, Miss Sophia was at her door, waiting for me. She was so glad to get that Bible that she grabbed me and gave me a good squeeze.

"You're the best boy in the world. But remember, don't tell anyone," she said. Her eyes lit up, which made her look even prettier.

"What's that paper all about?" I asked her.

"It's only a bookmark," she said.

I went off down the river, studying over what happened. I kept walking till I came to the swamp. I looked out at the moss and grass growing up from the water. Then I heard something rustling nearby.

I was extra careful as I went to see what was rustling. It could've just been a frog or a bird, but something told me that it was more. Sure enough, I was in for a surprise. There behind some vines I found a sleeping man. I'll be dogged if it wasn't Jim.

"Jim!" I yelled, waking him up.

"Huck!" He nearly cried when he saw me.

I was even happier to see him. "Jim, where have you been all this time?"

"I knew you were up at that house, so I've been sneaking around, watching what was going on. I was afraid to come too close. I spent my time here, trying to avoid the water moccasins."

"What are you going to do?"

Jim looked around the swamp. "Stay here for now."

I hated leaving him out there, but I knew I couldn't bring him up to the house. I needed to come up with a plan.

The next morning when I woke up, things were awfully quiet. I saw that even Buck had up and gone.

I went downstairs, but nobody was around. I walked outside, but nobody was out there either. When I got back in, the housekeeper was standing in the kitchen.

"What's going on?" I asked.

She shook her head, looking down at the floor. "Everybody's in an uproar," she said. "Miss Sophia has run away."

I couldn't believe it. I ran out and up the river as fast as I could. There was gunfire blasting a ways off.

When I got to the woodpile where the steamboats land, I climbed up an old cottonwood tree. I sat on one of the high branches to watch.

There was Buck and the Grangerford boys shooting across at the Shephersons.

"Buck!" I called.

He looked around, wondering where the voice was coming from.

"Buck!"

Then he looked up in the tree and saw me.

"What's all the fighting about?" I asked.

Buck loaded some more bullets in his rifle. "Sophia," he said. "She ran off with Harney Shepherdson. They made it across the river."

I was glad to hear that Miss Sophia was safe.

"I should have shot old Harney that day in the woods," Buck went on. "We wouldn't be having this trouble if I had."

All of a sudden, *Bang! Bang! Bang!* The gunfire started up again. I stayed up in the tree, afraid to come down. I wondered if I should've told Miss Sophia's father about that piece of paper. 'Cause then he would've locked her up, and all this wouldn't have happened.

When it got dark and quiet I finally came down. There were bodies everywhere. I tiptoed through, trying to make my way back. That's when I saw something that made me want to wail. Buck had been shot in the face.

I started crying, and bent down by his body. I took off my jacket and covered his face. It all seemed so useless.

I knew I couldn't go back to the house, so I made my way to the swamp and found Jim. I was never happier to see someone in my whole life. "Let's go," I told him.

Jim had gotten another raft for us, so I hopped on and we sailed away.

The King and the Duke

Two or three days went by. We'd ride the river at night and hide out during the day. Once or twice a night we'd see a steamboat. Then it would turn the corner and its lights would wink out, but its waves would still hit and joggle our raft a bit.

One night, I went up on the shore to pick some wild berries. That's when I saw a couple of men running. One looked to be about seventy, with a bald head and gray whiskers. The other had on a battered hat and a greasy blue shirt. Both of them were carrying ratty-looking carpet bags.

It scared me to death because when somebody's running that quick, I figure they're after Jim and me. I was about to hurry out of there when they started yelling.

"Save us," said one man.

"Save you from what?" I asked them.

"We weren't doing anything wrong, yet some men and their dogs started chasing us," the man with the hat said.

They wanted to jump onto the raft, but I said, "Wait. I don't hear dogs or horses yet. You have time to cut through the brush and head up a little ways. I'll meet you up there and then we can take off."

"Great idea," the bald man tells me.

Soon they were aboard, and it was five or ten minutes later before we heard the dogs. By then, we were long gone.

After breakfast those two men began talking. It turned out they didn't even know each other.

"What got you into trouble?" said the bald-headed man to the other.

"I'd been selling a potion that'll take tartar off of teeth. It works too, except it also takes the enamel off with it. I guess I stayed one night too many. I was heading out when I ran into you running like a fool. Since I was expecting trouble myself, I thought it was a good idea if we hightailed it together. What did you do?"

The younger man said, "I'd been preaching the word of God. Some of the women-folks particularly took to liking me. I was pulling in five or six dollars a night. Then it got out that I was spending way too much time drinking, and that maybe I wasn't a man of God after all. I knew if I got caught, they'd tar and feather me for sure."

No one said anything else for a while. Then the younger man said, "Alas, it's tragic that I should end up like this."

"What'd you mean?" I asked him.

"Here I am, wearing rags and riding on a raft, when I should be dressed in the best tailored suits and sailing on a steamboat."

The bald man rubbed his head. "And what makes you think you're any better than us?"

"Because of the secret of my birth," the younger one said. "By rights, I'm a duke!"

Jim's eyes bugged out when he heard that, and I reckon mine did, too.

"Yes," he went on. "My great-grandfather was the eldest son of the Duke of Bridgewater."

Jim and I both felt sorry for him. "That's awful," I said. "Should we address you as Your Grace, or My Lord, or Your Lordship?"

The man shook his head. "You can just call me by my title, Bridgewater. It's not right for me to serve myself though. I think someone should do that for me."

That was easy enough. All through dinner, Jim stood around and waited on him. Anybody could see that Bridgewater was pretty pleased.

But the old bald man got pretty silent. Then he said, "Looky here, Bilgewater. You aren't the only one with problems. I've also been snaked from my rightful place."

"You don't mean?" Bridgewater said.

"Yep," said the bald man. "You gentlemen are looking at the rightful King of France."

Well, he cried and took on so, Jim and I hardly knew what to do. We figured he deserved the same attention as the duke.

It didn't take me long to figure these liars weren't really a king and a duke. They were just a couple of low-down frauds. But I never let on. 'Cause there was one thing I did learn from Pap. To get along with this type of folks, it's best to let them have their own way.

The Wilks Family

After a while, the king and the duke got tired of only moving during the night. I explained that it was mostly because of Jim. We couldn't take a chance on him being seen.

Then the duke had an idea. When we came to a small town, we docked the raft and the duke set out looking for a printing shop. He brought back a piece of paper that said, *Runaway Slave. $300.00 Reward.*

"Now," the duke said. "If someone stops us during the day, we'll just show them this paper and say that we captured him.

I have to admit, that was a smart idea.

So we sailed out both night and day, and we kept passing town after town. Soon the king and the duke decided it was time to make some money. We waited on shore near a loading dock, and soon a steamboat came in. The duke wandered off while I stayed by the king.

We saw a fellow standing around, waiting, so the king went over and struck up a conversation with him. The man said, "I swear, when I first saw you, I thought you were Mr. Harvey Wilks. But then I figured you couldn't be him. You aren't, are you?"

"No," the king said, his ears perking up.

The man hung his head. "Poor Mr. Wilks. His brother, Peter, died last night. And he's going to miss the funeral."

"Where is Harvey Wilks?" the king asked.

"He's in Sheffield, England," the man said. "And it's such a shame. He only had two brothers, and now that Peter is gone, that only leaves George. And George is a deaf-mute."

The king seemed mighty interested in the Wilks family. He kept on asking questions. "Why isn't Harvey Wilks coming?"

"Well, about a month or two ago when Peter first got sick, he sent Harvey a letter. He asked Harvey to take over his property. And he let Harvey know there was money hidden. But, that letter might not have reached Harvey."

The king suddenly became real concerned. "Too bad, too bad. Are you going to the funeral?" he asked.

"I can't," the man tells him. "I'm going to be boarding a ship on Wednesday that's headed out of the country. But I wish I could pay my respects to Peter's three daughters. They're left all alone. The oldest, Mary Jane, is nineteen. Then there's Susan, who is fifteen. And the younger one, Joanna, is about fourteen."

The king shook his head. "Poor things." He went on talking for a good bit, pumping that man for more information. I knew what he was up to, but I didn't say a word.

After the man said he had to shove along, the king turned to me and said, "Run get the duke."

When I got back with the duke, they both sat down on a log. The king told him every word the man had said. And the whole time, he was trying to talk like an Englishman. He was pretty good at it, too.

"How are you at pretending to be deaf and mute?" he asked the duke.

The duke smiled at him. "Don't you worry."

So we made our way about five miles down where about a dozen men were standing about. Then the king asked, "Can any of you gentlemen tell me where Mr. Peter Wilks lives?"

One of them said softly and gently, "I'm sorry, sir, but we can only tell you were he did live. Peter died yesterday."

Well, that no good old king fell against the man and started blubbering like a baby. "Oh, my poor brother!" Then he turns to the duke and makes some signs with his hands, and I'll be darn if he didn't bust out crying, too.

The men gathered and sympathized with them. They even carried their carpet bags up the hill for them. The king and the duke leaned on the men's shoulders, still sobbing like crazy.

We made it up to the house, and out came Mary Jane with her pretty red hair and sad eyes. The king spread his arms and she ran to him. The younger girl ran to the duke, and they cried with joy to be meeting at last.

Then they peeked in and saw the coffin. Their heads drooped as they made their way over to it. And they were crying so loud I figured the whole town could hear them.

Soon more folks showed up. The reverend, the doctor, and a lawyer were among them. The king shook their hands and thanked them for coming. Of course the duke didn't say a word. He kept making all kinds of strange signs with his hands.

The king continued to blab on. He said that Peter had sent him letters. Of course it was all information he got from the fellow at the docks.

Then Mary Jane brought out a letter that her father never got a chance to send. The king read it out loud and cried some more. It said that Peter was leaving $3,000 to Harvey and William, and it told where another $6,000 was hidden in the cellar.

Naturally, these two old frauds said they'd go and get it. They told me to bring a candle, and we shut the cellar door behind us.

They ran their fingers through that gold, and let the coins jingle to the floor.

"Hey, I've got an idea," the duke said. "Let's take this money upstairs and give it to the girls."

The king seemed to know what the duke was planning. So they went upstairs and set the bag of money on the table. The king counted it out in front of everyone. Then he pointed to the girls and said, "These poor little lambs. They've suffered so much. I know what my brother would want me to do."

He turned to the duke and made those hand signs. The duke watched for minute, then his eyes brightened up like he'd finally caught on. He gave the king a big smile.

The king said, "Here, Mary Jane, Susan, and Joanna. Take the money. Take it all."

They all three started hugging him again. But the town doctor, who'd stood watching the whole time, stuck his finger in the king's face.

"You can't fool me!" he hollered. "You ain't nothing but a fraud!"

My heart thumped like a rabbit, and I thought we were caught for sure!

The Funeral

The king stood there, looking gap-jawed at the doctor. The doctor kept on yelling. "You claim you're an Englishman, but that's the worst English accent I've ever heard! You are nothing but a swindler."

The crowd gathered around the doctor, trying to quiet him down.

"No," one man argued. "It's really Harvey Wilks."

"Yeah," another agreed. "He knew everybody's name. He even knew all our dogs' names."

"I'm telling you," the doctor warned. "Anyone who can't imitate an accent better than that is a fraud."

The Wilks girls hung their heads and cried. That's when the doctor turned to them and said, "I was your father's friend. I only want to protect you and keep you out of trouble. He's an imposter who's come here with a lot of names and facts that he picked up somewhere else. Won't you please turn this rascal out?"

Mary Jane straightened up, looking proud. "Here is my answer to that." She picked up the bag of money and put it right in the king's hands. "Here," she said. "Take the whole $6,000 and invest it for me and my sisters."

Then she put her arm around the king on one side, and the other girls did the same on the other. Everyone clapped and stomped while the king held his head high.

The doctor pointed his finger at them. "Fine. But remember, I warned you."

After supper I started wondering what I ought to do. Should I go to that doctor and tell him the truth? I couldn't do that. The king and the duke might find out it was me, and they'd have my hide for sure. I knew Mary Jane wouldn't believe me.

I figured the only way to help those girls was to steal that money and hide it. Then when I'm off down the river, I could write to Mary Jane and tell her where it was.

I searched around the king's room. I could barely see anything without a candle. But then I heard footsteps. I jumped behind a curtain and waited. In walked the king and the duke.

"What are we going to do?" the duke asked.

"I think we should head out of here after everyone's asleep. That doctor's got me nervous. How about we sneak out around three in the morning?"

The duke agreed. "But we better put that money in a better spot so no one will find it."

That was a stroke of luck. Now I'd know where to find it. But then I worried. What if they decided to hide it behind the curtain? If they found me, I'd be in a heap of trouble.

But the king said, "Let's stick it in here."

I peeked out and saw them stuff that bag into a big hole in the mattress. Then they headed out.

I waited until they were halfway down the stairs, then grabbed that money and hurried back to my room. I started wondering where I could hide so the king and the duke wouldn't find it.

Late that night I took the money downstairs. I thought maybe it would be best to store it someplace outside, but then I heard someone coming in. I had to think fast.

So what did I do? I stuffed that money inside Peter Wilks's coffin! I flew out of there as quick as I could.

I didn't sleep much at all that night. I kept trying to figure a way to get that money out. When I went downstairs that morning, folks were already gathered around the coffin. Pretty soon the undertaker showed up, and he lowered the lid. I didn't dare lift it back up to see if the money was still there.

The funeral ceremony was good, but a bit long. And the king stood up and talked a bunch of rubbish about how he loved his brother, Peter. Everybody was crying and wailing. Then, before I knew it, the undertaker took out his screwdriver to seal the coffin lid.

I didn't know what to do. I figured I should just head out, then write to Mary Jane and tell her to dig up the coffin.

After the funeral, the king still hung around, acting like he was part of the family. He had to know that money was gone, but he carried on like nothing was wrong.

I slunk around, worrying how I was going to get away. The king and the duke both kept a close eye on me. I wondered if they knew I had taken the money.

But late that evening, something truly unexpected happened. In walked two gentlemen wearing fine clothes and shiny boots.

"We're here at last," one said in a proper English accent. "So sorry we are late, but our luggage was misplaced."

Everybody's jaws dropped. They knew that the two men who'd just arrived were the real Wilks brothers.

CHAPTER 14

Mistaken Identity

I didn't wait to see what happened next. I hightailed it out of there so fast they didn't even notice. I vowed to write that letter to Mary Jane just as soon as we were down the river.

I ran a good ways until I found the raft, but it was empty. There was no sign of Jim anywhere.

"Jim!" I yelled. "Jim!"

I looked around, wondering if he was in the river taking a swim. I ran this way and that, up and down the shore. He wasn't anywhere around. I plopped myself down and started worrying.

That's when a strange man walked up. He looked over at the raft, then at me. "You looking for that runaway slave?"

My heart dropped down to my toes. "Do you know where he is?"

The man nodded. "He was captured by one of the local farmers."

"Do you know which farm?" I kept my fingers crossed that he could answer.

"They were taking him to the Phelps's place."

"Where is it?" I asked nicely. And lucky for me, the man gave me directions.

It turns out, Phelps's place was just a small plantation with a rail fence and a tiny hut in the back. I went up to the door without a plan laid out. I wasn't sure what I was going to say.

Then out came a woman about fifty years old. "It's you, at last!" she bellowed. She threw her arms around me, and gave me a tight hug.

"You don't look as much like your mother as I thought you would," she said, looking me over. "But I'm just so glad to see you, Tom!"

I didn't know who Tom was, but I didn't mind letting her think I was him.

"Come on inside," she said. "Have something to eat. Nothing's too good for my nephew."

At least now I knew a little something about Tom. She sat me down in a chair and started asking me about my trip.

"Where's your baggage?"

"It's lost," I lied.

"Oh, that's a shame," she said. "I'm sure we'll find some clean clothes for you. So how is Sis?"

Now, I was really in trouble. What was I going to tell her? I didn't know a thing about her sister. Before I could make up a tale, in walks an old gentleman. I figured it must be Mr. Phelps.

"Who's that?" he asked.

"Well who else could it be?" Mrs. Phelps answered. "It's our nephew, Tom Sawyer!"

My jaw about dropped to the floor.

The old man grabbed me by the hand and

kept on shaking it. The whole time the woman danced around, laughing and crying. Then they started firing off questions about Sid and Mary and the rest of the family.

Nothing made me happier than to find out who I was supposed to be. I knew a lot about the Sawyer family, and spent hours catching them up on everything. But then I heard a steamboat coughing along the river.

I started worrying. What if Tom was on that boat? What if he walked in and called out my name? I had to get down there and warn him.

"I think I'll go look for my baggage," I said.

"Maybe I should come with you," Mr. Phelps suggested.

"No, I'll be fine."

Once I was out the door, I lit out, and headed toward town. I was halfway there when I saw a wagon coming my way. And sure enough, there sat Tom, riding high. His mouth formed an O, and his eyes bugged out.

"Stay away!" he hollered. "I ain't never done you no harm. Why are you coming back to haunt me?"

"I ain't coming back," I told him. "I've never been gone."

His eyebrows twitched and he scratched his head. "You ain't a ghost?"

"Nope. I'm not dead. I was never murdered. It was just a trick I played to get away. Here," I said, holding out my arm. "You can touch me and feel that I'm real."

He did, then his face broke into a smile. "Huck, it looks like you had your own adventure."

I told him all about it, and how Jim was somewhere on the farm.

"So now I'm in a real fix. And I need you to stay quiet about it, Tom, 'cause I'm planning to steal Jim away."

His eyes lit up. "I'll help you steal him."

"Are you joking?" I asked.

He crossed his heart and promised, "I'm not joking." Right then I knew things just might work out.

When we got back, Mr. and Mrs. Phelps looked awful puzzled. "Who do we have here?" Mrs. Phelps asked.

Tom didn't answer. He just went right up and gave her a big old kiss.

"Lands, boy!" she shouted, wiping her mouth with her apron. "Who do you think you are?"

Tom looked shocked and hurt. "Sorry, ma'am," he said, "but they told me you'd want a big kiss."

"Who told you that?" she asked.

"Everyone. They said when I see Aunt Sally, I should give her a big kiss."

Aunt Sally eyed him, looking him over good. Then a smile split her face. "Ah!" she screamed. "I wasn't expecting you!"

She looked over at Mr. Phelps and said, "Silas, come over here. It's Tom's brother, Sid Sawyer!"

Tom hugged them and carried on like he was Sid.

"Sis wrote to me saying that Tom was the only one coming," Aunt Sally said.

Tom shrugged. "Well, I didn't think it would be fair for Tom to come and not me. I begged and begged until she let me come, too."

"We're just glad that you're both here," Uncle Silas said.

Tom gave me a wink, and I started feeling a lot better about the whole situation.

After dinner, Tom and I went up to our room. Tom looked out to make sure no one was listening, then he said, "Huck, I think I know where they're keeping Jim."

I perked up fast. "Where?"

He walked over to the window and pointed out. He said, "I bet he's in that hut back there."

The Second Escape

"So here's the plan," I said. "We'll wait until the old man goes to sleep. Then, we'll steal the key out of his britches."

Tom scratched his chin like he was thinking hard. "Well, that plan would work, but it's mighty simple. What good is planning something that's too easy?"

I've known Tom Sawyer all my life, and he always had to turn things into an adventure. He came up with a new plan, and I agreed to it. I'd do anything to rescue Jim.

When everything was dark and still, we slipped down to the hut. We circled around, checking for ways in and out. Then I whispered through the slats, "Jim, are you in there?"

"Huck!" Jim called back. I could tell he was happy to hear my voice. "You came for me!"

"Yep," I said. "And Tom Sawyer is here, too."

"Can you boys get me out of here?"

I looked around and saw a window high up that had a board nailed across it. "I bet Jim would fit through there," I told Tom.

Tom just shook his head. "That's as easy as one, two, three. We need something that'll take twice as long. We ain't in any hurry."

We kept on looking, then Tom said, "We'll dig him out."

"Don't worry, Jim," I said. "We'll help you."

Tom and I went back for some shovels and set to work. It took awhile, but we dug a tunnel under the hut.

When we broke through, we climbed through and looked around. There sat Jim on an old splintered bed. His foot was chained to the bedpost. He was covered in sweat, but he looked happy.

"Now, get me loose," he said.

Tom pointed to the chain. "We need a saw."

I noticed that the end of the chain was just a large ring under the post. "We can just lift the bed, and slip the chain out."

Tom squinted his eyes at me. "No, Huck, that's too simple. We need to saw it loose."

Just then there was a commotion outside. Tom and I slunk out through the hole, kicked some dirt over it, and headed back.

I didn't get much sleep that night. I knew Tom wanted to make this an adventure, but the sooner we got Jim out the better.

When we sat down to breakfast the next morning, I was thinking of ways to sneak back to that hut and start sawing Jim loose.

Aunt Sally poured out some coffee, and then said to Uncle Silas, "Did you ever get a reply from that flyer on the runaway slave?"

My ears perked up like a hunting dog. Tom looked interested, too.

"No," Uncle Silas answered, "I just went ahead and put an ad in the newspapers in New Orleans and St. Louis. Hopefully, whoever owns him will get in touch."

My knees started quaking under the table. This was the worst news yet. If Miss Watson found Jim, she'd sell him off to someone in New Orleans. I just couldn't let that happen.

We waited throughout the day. Aunt Sally kept us busy, and Uncle Silas seemed to always have his eye on us. I wasn't sure when we'd get our chance to free Jim.

It was later that night when we got a lucky break. Some men showed up to visit Uncle Silas. They were talking and laughing, and I motioned for Tom to meet me by the back door. We hightailed it out, grabbed a hacksaw, and shimmied in through that hole in the hut.

"You came back!" Jim said. I never saw any human look so happy to see me.

"Yep. We need to get you out of here," I said. I didn't waste a moment sawing that bedpost.

"No!" Tom said, grabbing the saw from me. "That's not the way they do it in the books."

I knew Tom would think of something more complicated.

"We should saw his leg off instead."

More sweat beaded on Jim's face, and his eyes grew twice as big.

"That'll take too long, Tom. We need to get Jim out now."

That's when we heard a noise outside. "We better get busy!" I said. I sawed and sawed until that wooden bedpost was cut clean through. The sounds outside got closer.

"Let's go," Tom whispered.

We snaked our way out and took off running.

"He's getting away!" one man shouted.

We didn't bother looking back. We just kept running like our feet were on fire. We made it to the fence and hopped over, but that's when a gunshot rang by my ear. Tom fell over and hit the ground.

I couldn't believe it! He'd been shot!

Fetching the Doctor

"Keep going!" Tom urged, blood dripping down his leg. He ran behind us as we headed for the river. Once we were on the raft, we lay down, out of breath.

"That was close," I said.

Jim wiped some of the sweat from his forehead. "That was a mighty good job you boys did. Nobody could've done it better."

Tom was smiling and holding his leg. "And look! I took a bullet for the effort."

I've never heard of anyone being happy about getting shot, but Tom figured it as part of the adventure.

We laid him down inside the wigwam. Then, we found one of the duke's old shirts and tore it into strips for bandages. Tom held out his hand.

"Give me those," he said. "I can do it myself." He took the rags and tied them around his leg.

Jim motioned me out. "We can't just leave Tom like this. He needs a doctor."

I nodded and went back into the wigwam. "Hey, Tom," I said, "I think maybe we should find a doctor to remove that bullet."

"Are you crazy? I don't need no doctor!"

"You'll bleed to death," I pointed out.

"Then I'll die a hero," he said.

"No, you won't!"

As soon as the raft sailed down to the next village, we tied it to a tree limb, and I went straight to the town doctor. He was an old, kind-looking fellow.

"Come quick. My brother's been shot!"

The doctor lifted an eyebrow, and his eyes narrowed. "Who shot him?"

I had to make up another whopper of a lie. "He did."

"He shot himself?" the doctor asked.

"We went out hunting, and decided to take a nap on our raft. While we were dozing, he had an awful dream. It startled him so much, he kicked the gun. It went off and shot him in the leg."

"That must've been one powerful dream," the doctor said.

"Yes, sir. And we need you to come patch him up, but don't say nothing because we were planning to surprise our folks."

"Who are your folks?" he asked.

"The Phelpses. They live over yonder." I pointed in the direction of the town.

He lit his lantern and grabbed his saddlebags. When we got to the raft, I didn't see Jim at all. I figured he was hiding, because he was just too smart to get caught again.

The doctor went into the wigwam, and I found a spot under a willow tree to lie down. It was probably midnight or later, and I was tuckered out. Next thing I knew, I was asleep.

When I woke up the sun was high over my head! I didn't see anyone on the raft, so I shot up and went straight to the doctor's house.

A woman answered the door.

"Where's the doctor?" I asked.

"Why, he left sometime in the night. He hasn't come back."

I couldn't believe what I was hearing. Where was Tom? Where was Jim?

"Thanks!" I said, pushing out of there as quick as a jackrabbit. But I didn't make it far when I ran right into Uncle Silas!

"Why, Tom," he said. "Where have you been all this time, you rascal?"

It took me a minute to think about who I was. Uncle Silas still thought I was Tom.

"I was looking for that runaway slave," I told him.

"Well, your aunt's been beside herself with worry. Where's Sid?"

I shrugged. "It beats me."

"Let's get home," he said. "Aunt Sally's waiting. I bet Sid will show up soon."

As soon as I stepped into the house, Aunt Sally grabbed me up and hugged me tight. "We were worried when you weren't in your room last night," she told me. Then she looked behind me. "Where's Sid?"

I felt bad for making her worry so much. But I was worrying, too. I just wish I knew where Tom was. "Maybe I should go back into town and look for him."

"You'll do no such thing!" she ordered.

Well, I was stuck then. The best I could do was wait it out.

After supper, Tom still hadn't showed. "Where is that boy?" Aunt Sally worried.

"Now, stop your fretting," Uncle Silas said. "Boys will be boys. We'll just leave a candle burning in the window for him."

That didn't stop Aunt Sally from carrying on something awful. At bedtime she insisted on tucking me in.

"I'm so worried about Sid," she told me. "But at least you're safe. Promise me you'll stay right here and not leave this house."

When I didn't say anything, she continued, "For my sake, please promise you won't go out."

What could I do? I had to promise. And as much as I wanted to sneak through that window and look for Tom, I just couldn't upset Aunt Sally anymore.

With both Aunt Sally and Tom on my mind, I was restless all night. I crept out the window anyway, deciding not to go out of the yard. When I slipped around, I saw her sitting by the window with her eyes toward the road. It made me feel so bad, I decided right then that I would never do anything to upset her.

I went back into my room and slept for a bit. Around dawn I got up again. Aunt Sally was still at that window. Her candle had mostly burned out, but her old gray head was resting on her hand and she was sound asleep.

CHAPTER 17

Going Back

Aunt Sally and Uncle Silas were still fretting at breakfast. They both sat at the table, not saying a word. Then Aunt Sally looked out toward the window. "Sid!" she cried.

I looked up, and sure enough, it was Tom. He was being carried on a mattress by a group of men. The old doctor was walking right beside him. And so was Jim with his hands tied behind his back.

Aunt Sally ran outside. "Sid! Oh no, he's dead!" But then Tom stirred a little and she yelled again. "He's alive! Thank goodness!"

The doctor and Uncle Silas followed as they brought Tom into the house, but I stayed behind to see what they were going to do with

Jim. Those men pushed and shoved and bullied him all the way to the hut. They filled in the hole we'd dug. I was about ready to cry. We'd done all that rescuing for nothing.

I went back in to check on Tom. He was half asleep, but he kept muttering a lot of gibberish. When Aunt Sally put a cool rag to his head, he opened his eyes and smiled.

"It worked," he said.

"What worked?" Aunt Sally asked him.

"Our plan." Then he looked at me. "Didn't you tell Auntie the whole thing?"

Before I could answer, she said, "What whole thing?" Her eyes narrowed.

"About how we set Jim free."

Aunt Sally shook her head. "No, Sid. He was caught. They took him back to the hut."

Tom sat up, looking grave. "But you don't have any right locking him up! He's a free man."

"Now, you just get some rest, Sid," Aunt Sally said. "You need to clear your head."

"No!" Tom said. "I'm telling the truth. Old Miss Watson died two months ago, and she put in her will that she was setting him free."

Aunt Sally looked puzzled. "Then why on earth would you help him escape if he was already free?"

"That's a good question," said another woman who'd stepped into the room.

I knew I was in trouble now. It was Tom's Aunt Polly! I ditched under the bed as quick as I could.

Aunt Sally jumped up and gave her a hug. "I didn't know you were coming!"

Aunt Polly hugged her back, then said, "Mercy, Tom! You are always getting yourself in a scrape."

"What?" Aunt Sally said, scratching her head. "That ain't Tom, that's Sid."

Aunt Polly laughed. "I've raised that boy since he was a baby. That's Tom Sawyer."

"But Tom was right here a minute ago. Where'd Tom go?"

Aunt Polly looked over her spectacles, and tapped her foot. "You mean where did Huck Finn go. Come out, Huck."

I knew I was caught, so I slithered out from under the bed. Aunt Sally looked so mixed up her eyes were bobbing. Tom and I told her the truth about what happened.

Then Aunt Polly said, "Tom was right about Jim. Miss Watson did set him free."

Aunt Sally turned to us. "So you went through all that trouble to sneak away a slave that was already free?"

Tom shrugged. "It was an adventure."

We had Jim out of those chains in no time. And when Aunt Polly, Uncle Silas, and Aunt Sally found out how well he'd helped the doctor nurse Tom, they made a big fuss over him. They served him a plate full of food, and gave him forty dollars as a reward.

After a few days, Tom and Jim and I talked about leaving. "I need to collect some of my money from Judge Thatcher," Tom said.

I felt a tinge as my blood ran cold. "The money! I can't go back, Tom. I bet Pap has already taken all my money. No telling what he'll do to me."

"You don't have to worry about him," Jim said. "He won't bother you ever again."

"How do you know that?" I asked him.

Jim hung his head a little. "Remember that house that was caught up on the river? Remember the dead man inside? I covered his face so you couldn't see, Huck. It was your pappy that was lying there. He likely got into trouble for cheating at poker."

I probably should've been sad, but I wasn't. I could go back now without any worries at all.

So there. That's all I have to write about. And I'm rotten glad, too. Writing a book isn't all that easy.

And besides, I need to get away quick. Aunt Sally's talking about adopting me, and I don't think I could stand to be "civilized" again. I've been there before!